BUG SAFARI

Bob Barner

Holiday House / New York

The art in this book was done with cut and torn paper from around
the world as well as paste paper made by the author and his wife.
The text typeface is Memphis Medium.
www.holidayhouse.com

3 5 7 9 10 8 6 4 2

Library of Congress Cataloging-in-Publication Data
Barner, Bob.
Bug safari / Bob Barner.—1st ed.
p. cm.
Summary: Tells how the author, as a young boy, followed
a trail of ants and came across various other insects and small
creatures, then briefly provides facts about each
creature encountered.
ISBN 0-8234-1707-7 (hardcover)
1. Insects—Juvenile literature. [1. Insects.] I. Title.

QL467.2.B364 2004
595.7—dc22
2003056619

Designed by Yvette Lenhart

ISBN-13: 978-0-8234-1707-0 (hardcover)
ISBN-13: 978-0-8234-2038-4 (paperback)

ISBN-10: 0-8234-1707-7 (hardcover)
ISBN-10: 0-8234-2038-8 (paperback)

To Mary Meeham,
who never
bugs me

The events described here actually happened to me.

The things I learned are recorded to the best of my memory. We can still observe and learn from the great, great ancestors of the very ants I saw that day so very long ago— well, last summer.

I was lost in a bug-infested jungle one hot summer day. I was all alone, looking for a way back to base camp, when I saw a long line of marching black ants. Where could they be going? It looked like an ant safari. Was this a way out of the jungle?

I decided to follow.

In all of my travels I had never seen anything like the ant safari. Some of the ants carried things to eat such as leaves, seeds, or bits of other insects. The ant safari was in a hurry to get somewhere. The ants didn't even look up at the big dragonfly that buzzed over our heads. We headed deeper into the dark unknown jungle.

I crawled over rocks and through mud. I had to find out where the ants were going. The safari passed under flowers that were humming with honeybees collecting pollen.

I was measuring one of the ants with my ruler when the other ants zoomed past me and a slow-moving dung beetle. I noticed that the ants talked to one another by touching antennae on top of their heads. They all knew where they were going. We were moving quickly—but to where and what?

Then I saw them up ahead. Red ants. The black ants were fighting them. The tiny red ants were fierce and bit the black ants. The black ants stood their ground and battled for several minutes until the outnumbered red ants finally ran away. One of the black ants took charge. I called it the general. The wounded were treated and the safari continued.

I was baking in the sun. I had a drink from my canteen. Just one sip left. The ants became very excited. They had come upon a toad sitting in the middle of their path. Most of the ants ran around it, but a few of them got zapped. Why would they keep going with all of this danger? Where could they be going?

Then I saw it. A giant green mantis in the bush above the ants. One of the ants was plucked up and eaten. But all of the others marched ahead. They passed under sticky spiderwebs, spotted beetles, and noisy crickets that made a chirping noise as we passed by. I picked my way through the jungle. I had scraped my knees and cut my finger, and needed medical attention. I bravely pressed onward, hoping I would one day see another human being.

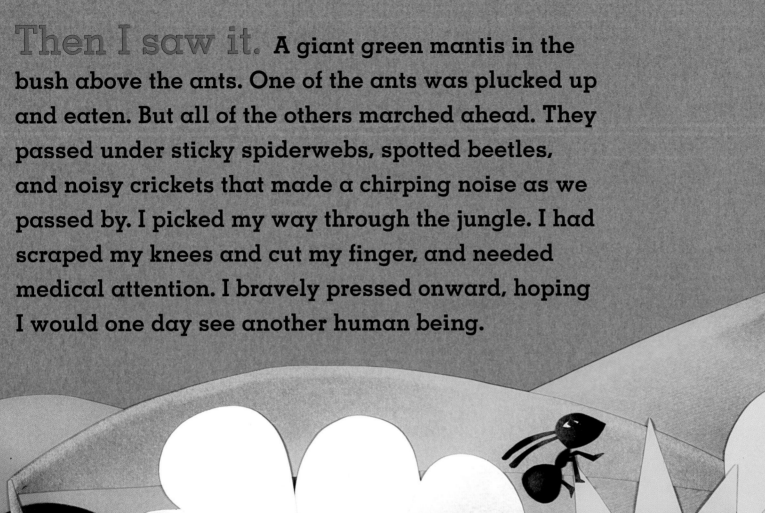

All of a sudden a hairy black spider pounced in front of the ants! The general led the safari around the giant, but I feared the worst. I hid my eyes and ducked for cover. Then, with a swooshing sound, the spider was gone. I looked up to see its eight legs wiggling in the beak of a robin. We were all safe for the moment. The general marched on.

I was out of water, famished, and covered with bites. Then I heard a faint sound in the distance. I was perfectly still in the brush so I could listen very carefully. A lone mosquito buzzed past my ear. Finally, I heard the call. A human voice.

Base camp!

Lunch was ready. To my surprise I discovered where the ants were going.

I love a good safari.

And so do the ants.

Bugs in the Book

Most of the creatures in this book are insects. An insect has three body parts: a head, an abdomen, and a thorax. These three parts are easy to see in an ant but harder to see in insects such as ladybugs or walking sticks. All insects also have six legs.

Bug is a word used to describe many small creatures. See if you can guess which two bugs on this page are not insects.

Cricket Field crickets are common all over North America. Crickets make a musical sound by rubbing their forewings together.

Dung Beetle A dung beetle, or tumblebug, lays one egg in a ball of dung it has collected. Then it buries the ball in the ground. When the larva hatches, it eats the dung.

Stag Beetle Only the male stag beetle has big jaws. The beetles use their big jaws in fights. The female lays its eggs in decaying wood, and the larvae eat it after hatching.

Centipedes are arthropods not insects. Arthropods have bodies with many sections and two legs on each section. Most centipedes are active at night and hide under stones or leaves during the day.

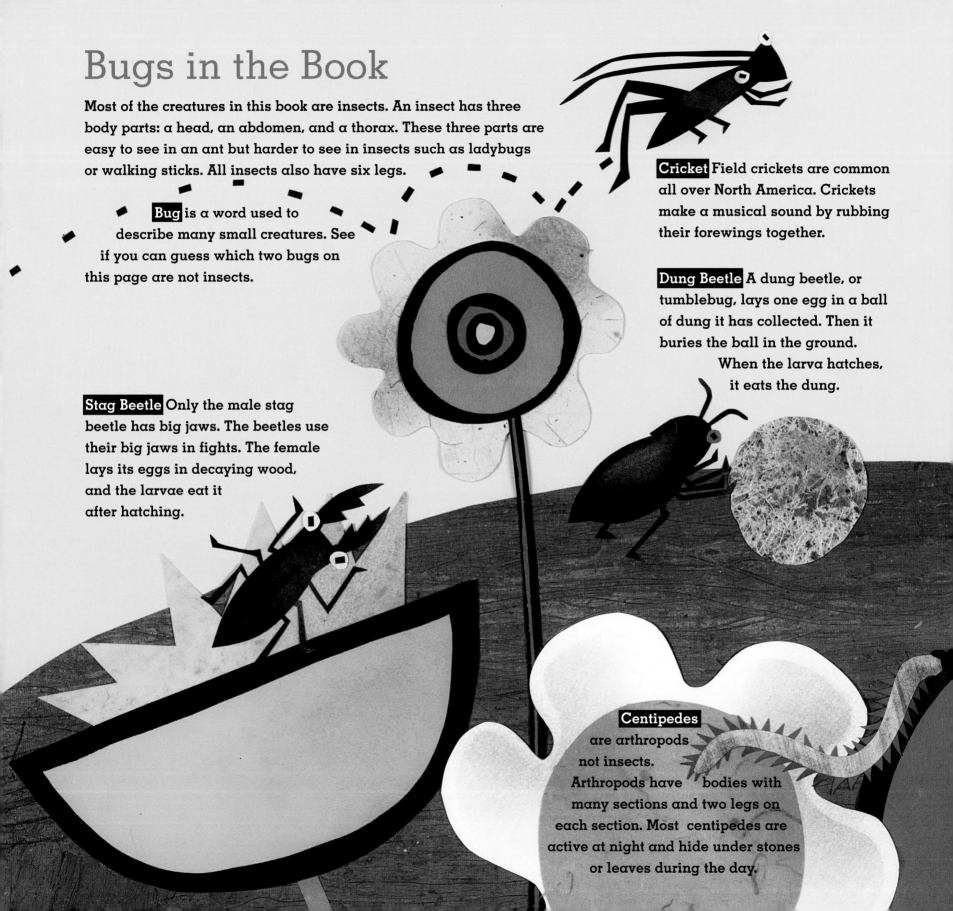

Mosquito You can usually hear a mosquito before you see it. The males feed on honeydew from plants, but the females feed on blood.

Stinkbug Stay away from stinkbugs. They can make a very stinky fluid to scare away enemies. The strong smell can stain your skin or even cause a headache.

Spider A spider is an arachnid not an insect. An arachnid has two body parts, eight legs, no wings, and no antennae. Many spiders catch bugs in their webs for food. Spiders come in lots of sizes, from tiny to about 10 inches in diameter. Most spiders have eight eyes.

Butterfly A butterfly is a caterpillar all grown up. You can see butterflies on almost any sunny day drinking the nectar from flowers. The smallest butterflies have a wingspan of only about 1/2 inch. The largest have wingspans of more than 12 inches.

Honeybee Honeybees live in colonies in hollow trees. They turn pollen and nectar they collect from flowers into honey.

Mantis The mantis holds its front legs together so it looks as if it is praying. That's why it is sometimes called a praying mantis. The mantis is a very quick hunter. It can snatch other bugs right out of the air as they fly by.

Caterpillar A caterpillar is a moth or butterfly waiting to be born. These larvae hatch from eggs and do almost nothing but eat until they form a chrysalis from which the adult moth or butterfly will come. Be careful. Some caterpillars can make skin itch or burn when they are touched.

Dragonfly Dragonflies can have wings more than 4 inches wide. They fly around wet areas and catch other insects for food.

Fly Flies are expert fliers and can move quickly. Some kinds can even take off backward or sideways. Flies cannot chew and must drink all their food.

Walking Stick Walking sticks look like twigs or leaves with legs. Most of these large insects do not have wings. Their six legs are all about the same length. These slow-moving bugs like to eat leaves.

Ladybug There are many types of beetles. Ladybugs are the most well known. Ladybugs come in many colors. Each ladybug can have from two to twenty-four spots.

Ant The first ant appeared 130 million years ago. Ants come in many colors and range in size from 1/6 to 3/4 inch long. The ants we see above ground are usually worker and soldier ants. Only male ants and queens have wings. Only queen ants lay eggs. Ants live in large groups called colonies either underground or sometimes above ground in piles of loose leaves or rotten wood. Some ants bite; others sting. Ants have jaws called mandibles that they use to crunch food or to fight other insects. Ants may eat plants, insects, or both. Ants can talk to one another by touching antennae.